W9-AOC-246

Growing Vegetable Soup

Written and illustrated by Lois Ehlert

Voyager Books
Harcourt Brace & Company
San Diego   New York   London

DEDICATED TO MY FELLOW GARDENERS:
GLADYS, HARRY, JOHN, AND JAN

Requests for permission to make copies of any part of the
work should be mailed to: Permissions Department,
Harcourt Brace & Company, 6277 Sea Harbor Drive,
Orlando, Florida 32887-6777.

Voyager Books is a registered trademark of
Harcourt Brace & Company.

Library of Congress Cataloging-in-Publication Data

Ehlert, Lois.
Growing vegetable soup.
"Voyager Books."

Summary: A father and child grow vegetables and then
make them into a soup.

[1. Vegetable gardening—Fiction.   2. Soups—Fiction.]
I. Title.
PZ7.E44Gr   1987   [E]   86-22812
ISBN 0-15-232575-1
ISBN 0-15-232580-8 pb
ISBN 0-15-232581-6 oversize pb

P O N M

Printed in Singapore

Dad says we are going to grow vegetable soup.

rake

shovel

hoe

We're ready to work, and our tools are ready, too.

We are planting

seed package

soil

hole

the seeds,

garden glove

green bean
seed

pea
seed

corn
seed

zucchini squash
seed

carrot
seeds

and all the sprouts,

broccoli

potato eyes

trowel

PEPPER

CABBAGE

set onions

peat moss pot

TOMATO

POTATO

GREEN BEAN

CARROT

CABBAGE

watering can

and giving them water,

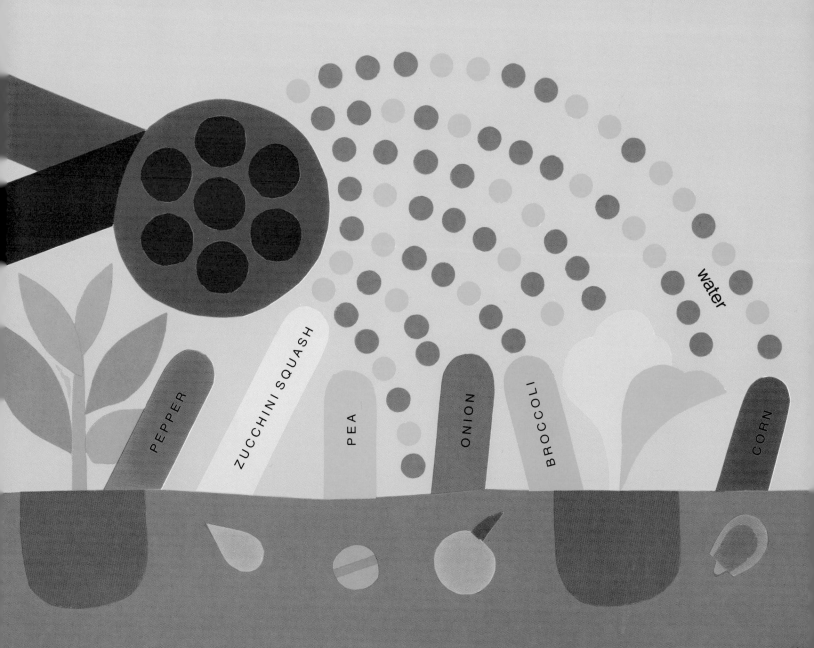

and waiting for warm sun to make them grow,

and grow,

soil

ZUCCHINI SQUASH

ONION

POTATO

PEA

CARROT

CORN

weed

and grow into plants.

squash
bud

ZUCCHINI SQUASH

squash
blossom

We watch

worm

BROCCOLI

over them and weed,

until the vegetables
are ready for us
to pick

TOMATO

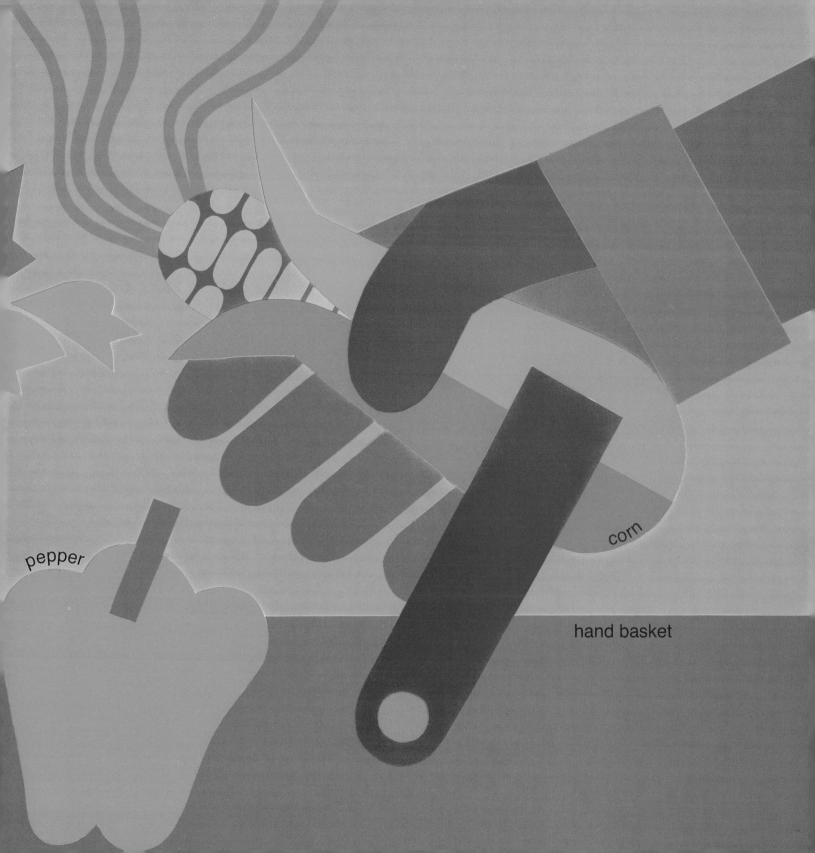

pepper

corn

hand basket

spading
fork

or dig up

carrot

potato

bushel basket

and carry home.
Then we wash them

cabbage

onion

pail

and cut them and put them in a pot of water,

soup pot

soup ladle

and cook them into vegetable soup!

steam

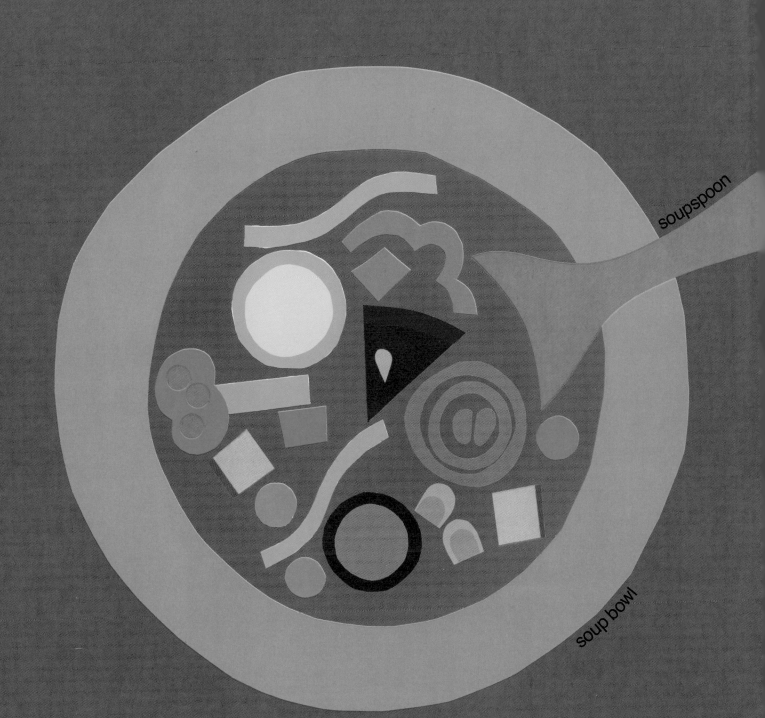

soupspoon

soup bowl

At last it's time
to eat it all up!

It was the
best soup ever...

and we can grow it again next year.